THE
SUPER BOWL

MATT CHRISTOPHER®

The #1 Sports Series for Kids

★ LEGENDARY SPORTS EVENTS ★

THE
SUPER BOWL

LITTLE, BROWN AND COMPANY

New York ∽ Boston ∽ London

Little, Brown and Company

Hachette Book Group USA
1271 Avenue of the Americas, New York, NY 10020
Visit our Web site at www.lb-kids.com

www.mattchristopher.com

First Edition: November 2006

Matt Christopher® is a registered trademark of
Matt Christopher Royalties, Inc.

Text written by Stephanie Peters

Library of Congress Cataloging-in-Publication Data

Christopher, Matt.
  Super Bowl! : 40 years of championship history / Matt Christopher ; [text writ-
ten by Stephanie Peters].— 1st ed.
      p. cm.
  Includes bibliographical references and index.
  ISBN-13: 978-0-316-01116-7 (pbk. : alk. paper)
  ISBN-10: 0-316-01116-9 (pbk. : alk. paper)
  1. Super Bowl—History—Juvenile literature. I. Peters, Stephanie True,
1965- II. Title.
GV956.2.S8C487 2005
796.332'648—dc22

                                                        2005030098

10 9 8 7 6 5 4 3 2 1

COM-MO

Printed in the United States of America

Contents

Chapter One: 1869–1967   1
The Pre–Super Bowl Century

Chapter Two: 1967–1968   6
Vince Lombardi and the Green Bay Packers

Chapter Three: 1969   16
Broadway Joe

Chapter Four: 1970–1974   24
Colts, Cowboys, Dophins . . . and Dolphins

Chapter Five: 1975–1976   34
The Steelers Steal the Show

Chapter Six: 1977–1980   40
Steelers Again!

Chapter Seven: 1981–1986   49
Rising Quarterbacks and Super-Powered Defenses

Chapter Eight: 1987–1988   58
Bucking the Broncos

Chapter Nine: 1989–1990   66
Return of the 49ers

Chapter Ten: 1991–1996   73
Repeat Defeats and the Rise of a New Dynasty

Chapter Eleven: 1995–1999   80
Battles for Dynastic Supremacy

Chapter Twelve: 2000–2006   92
Into the New Millennium

THE
SUPER BOWL

⋆ CHAPTER ONE ⋆

1869–1967

The Pre–Super Bowl Century

According to sports lore, the Super Bowl — the most-watched football game in the world — got its name from a child's toy.

The first Super Bowl was called the AFL-NFL World Championship Game. The people in charge of the leagues agreed that that name wasn't terribly exciting.

"In our discussions, we kept referring to it as the 'final game' or the 'championship game' or whatever, but it was awkward," recalled Lamar Hunt, then owner of the Kansas City Chiefs and creator of the American Football League (AFL). Then Hunt saw his daughter playing with a small, high-bouncing rubber ball — a Super Ball.

"One day I happened to say, 'When we get to the

super bowl . . . ,' and everyone knew what I was talking about," Hunt said.

The name stuck. Today, the Super Bowl is watched on television by millions of people worldwide. It wasn't always so popular, however. In fact, professional football in general had to earn its place in the sports world.

Sports historians mark November 6, 1869, as the first football game — despite the fact that the match was more a rough-and-tumble combination of soccer and rugby. Teams were made up of twenty-five players: two guarding the goal line, eleven lined up as defense, and the remaining twelve working the offense. Players were not permitted to run with or throw the round ball, only to kick or push it forward with their hands, feet, heads, and bodies. Bodies were also used to break up any plays the opposite team was forming — the precursors of today's tackles. One point was scored every time the ball went over the goal line.

This first football game was played at the college level between Rutgers University and Princeton University. At the end of the game, Rutgers had put the ball across six times, Princeton only four.

In the years that followed, other colleges became interested in the new game and formed teams. As the sport spread across the country, the rules of play began to evolve. By the late 1800s players were running with the ball, and tackling and blocking were a regular part of the game. A system of downs and yardage gains and losses was developed. The one-point goal was replaced with the four-point touchdown.

By this time, athletic clubs were offering non-college amateurs a chance to play. Before long, they began paying talented individuals to play for their squads, and then entire teams. Football was going professional.

By the turn of the century there were enough professional teams to form official football leagues. In 1920, the American Professional Football Association (APFA) was created in an effort to bring all the leagues together under one umbrella of rules and regulations. The Association officially changed its name to the National Football League in 1922.

Despite the increasing interest in the game, professional football struggled to gain a solid foothold in the world of sport. While attendance rose in some stadiums in the 1920s and 1930s, something needed to happen for football to capture the attention of sports fans nationwide.

That something happened at 2:30 p.m. on October 22, 1939. That day the National Broadcasting Company (NBC) televised an NFL game to approximately one thousand households. As television technology became more readily available around the country, more fans began watching games without leaving the comfort of their homes. By the late 1950s, hundreds of thousands of people were tuning in to see their favorite teams compete.

Spurred by this newfound and ever-increasing audience, a new football league, the American Football League (AFL), was formed in 1959. Created to rival the NFL, the AFL introduced a more open and exciting style of play. Attendance at and television ratings for AFL games skyrocketed as fans tuned in to see their favorite athletes play this thrilling kind of football.

Some NFL team owners wanted to stop the AFL, but others realized that it might be better to work with, rather than against, their competition. One such person was Pete Rozelle, commissioner of the

NFL. In the spring of 1966, he approached the AFL with a proposal to merge the two leagues into one. The AFL agreed and on June 8, 1966, the merger was announced.

Twenty-four teams, all original members of either the NFL or the AFL, made up the merged league. For the next few years, the AFL teams would play a separate schedule from the NFL teams. However, in the spirit of friendly competition, the top AFL team and the top NFL team would play a championship game at the end of the season.

And so it was that on January 15, 1967, football fans watched the first-ever Super Bowl.

☆ CHAPTER TWO ☆

1967–1968

Vince Lombardi and the Green Bay Packers

In 1958, the Green Bay Packers were one of the worst teams in the NFL. That year, they ended the season having won only one game out of thirteen. The previous years hadn't been much better. Football fans considered the Packers a loser team, scarcely worth watching.

One year later, however, the Packers' 1959 record stood at seven wins, five losses, and those same fans were paying much more attention to the Wisconsin team. The journey up from the cellar was due to the team's new head coach, Vince Lombardi.

Today, Vince Lombardi is considered a football legend. But in 1959, no one, least of all the players, knew what he would be like as a coach.

They found out quickly enough.

"I demand a commitment to excellence and to

victory," Lombardi let his players know. He expected them to give one hundred percent all the time, during games and practices. "Do it again until we get it right," he said when a play didn't go as planned.

Lombardi recognized that the Packers had plenty of talented players. He believed they just needed discipline and innovative plays to become a great team. So that's what he gave them.

Under Lombardi's direction, the Packers rose to become the top team in the NFL. From 1959 to 1966, they won the NFL championship title four times. And with a 1966 season record of 12 and 2, they earned the right to play in the first AFL-NFL World Championship Game.

The Packers' opponents were the Kansas City Chiefs. Owned by Lamar Hunt, the man who created the AFL in 1960, the team had a record of 11–2–1, more than good enough to seal their spot in the AFL-NFL match.

The first Super Bowl game was held on January 15, 1967, in Los Angeles's Memorial Coliseum. Tickets to the event cost ten dollars. Unlike today's Super Bowls, the game was not a sellout; still, close to 62,000 fans sat in the stands and an estimated 60 million viewers tuned in at home to see the much-hyped match.

One person who was looking forward to watching the event was Max McGee. McGee had once been a favorite receiver of Green Bay quarterback Bart Starr. But that year he'd had a less-than-stellar season, catching only three passes. His chances of seeing any action that day seemed slim.

"I had no earthly idea I'd play in that game," McGee later wrote.

But early in the first quarter, Packer wide receiver Boyd Dowler injured his shoulder. "McGee," Lombardi shouted to his second-stringer, "get in the game!"

Once McGee was in position, play resumed. The Packers moved the ball down the field to the Kansas City 37-yard line. It was third and three. Quarterback Bart Starr took the snap and faded back. McGee, meanwhile, hustled down the field, crossing the 30-yard line, then the 20. Starr spotted him in the clear near the 19-yard line and spiraled a pass.

The ball came in a little behind McGee. But with a twist of his body, he got his right hand on it and gathered it in. "When the ball stuck I almost fainted," he later recalled.

Instead, he barreled toward the end zone for the first six points of the game. One kick later, the Packers were ahead, 7–0.

But the Chiefs weren't about to roll over just yet. Early in the second quarter, quarterback Len Dawson threw a seven-yard pass over the goal line into the waiting hands of running back Curtis McClinton. The extra point was good, and the game was tied.

But not for long. Starr powered the Packers down the field until they were in scoring position. Then he handed off to Jim Taylor. Taylor put his shoulder down, charged headlong into and through the Chiefs' defense, and crossed the line for six more points. Again, the extra-point kick soared through the uprights and the Packers were up by seven.

Still, the Chiefs were not ready to give up. Just before halftime, kicker Mike Mercer booted the ball 31 yards for a three-point field goal. Suddenly the score was a lot closer.

After the half, Coach Lombardi told his team that unless they took the wind out of Kansas City's sails, they would be beaten. Green Bay was the better team, he reminded them. Defeat would be shameful.

The Packers took their coach's words to heart. When play resumed, they went on the attack. Their primary target was the Chiefs' quarterback. In the first half, they had put pressure on Dawson with a four-man rush. Now they charged with a full-on blitz.

Their strategy worked. Dawson was sacked three times for losses. When the Packers came at him a fourth time, he threw the ball rather than suffer another loss.

That was a mistake. The shaky pass was picked off by Packer Willie Wood. Wood carried it 50 yards to the Chiefs' 5-yard line. On the next play, Elijah Pitts danced into the end zone behind a wall of Green Bay blockers. The extra point kick was good, and the score zoomed to 21–10.

"That interception gave them the momentum," Len Dawson later commented. "They took the ball and shoved it down our throats."

The Packers scored one more touchdown in the third quarter when Bart Starr found Max McGee two times for gains of 11 and 16, and then a third time for 13 yards and six points. Their last touchdown came in the fourth quarter and was a spectacular 80-yard march that ended with Pitts surging over the line from the one.

When the final gun sounded, the score stood at Packers 35, Chiefs 10.

After the game, Lombardi praised his team and players, particularly McGee and Starr. "What can you say about a guy like McGee. This was one of his finest games. And Bart called a perfect game, but that's not new."

In the months that followed the first Super Bowl, pro football continued to expand and gain in popularity. Once again Lombardi's Packers emerged on top. Their season ended with a victory over the Dallas Cowboys in the NFL Championships — a game better known by its nickname, the Ice Bowl. Played on December 31, 1967, in Green Bay, the temperature was 13 below freezing, with a wind chill of 45 below! It was so cold that officials couldn't use their whistles because the metal froze to their lips.

As unbelievable as the cold was, it was the game's final moments that sealed it as one of the most memorable in football's history. With less than a minute to go, the score was Cowboys 17, Packers 14.

Green Bay had the ball on Dallas's 1-yard line. Typical football strategy called for Bart Starr to hand the ball off. Instead, Starr chose to execute a quarterback sneak. He whispered his intentions to guard Jerry Kramer. Kramer knew what he had to do: open a hole and hope Starr could lunge through it with the ball.

The play couldn't have gone better. With sixteen seconds to go, Kramer flattened his man and Starr bulled his way across for the touchdown. The Packers were on their way to Super Bowl II!

Meanwhile, in the AFL, the Oakland Raiders had powered their way to first place with a 13–1 record and then clinched their spot in the Super Bowl with an easy 40–7 victory over the Houston Oilers.

The second AFL-NFL World Championship Game was scheduled to be played in Miami on January 14, 1968. Unlike the previous year, when the stands in the Los Angeles stadium were little more than half full, this outing was a sellout.

The Raiders were a team of hungry youngsters looking to make their mark. The Packers, on the other hand, had many players who were winding down their careers. While those players were experienced, some football followers wondered if the Packers had it in them to win.

But Green Bay was determined to emerge victorious, for two reasons. One, they wanted to defend their championship title. And two, they wanted to give Vince Lombardi the best retirement gift they could.

The Thursday before the championship, Lombardi had let the team know of his plans. "[He] told us how much he had enjoyed coaching us and how proud he was of us," Starr recalled. "We all had lumps in our throats. He was proud of us, but we were just as proud of him." And the team was determined to make him proud of them one last time by winning the AFL-NFL game.

In the match's opening minutes both teams struggled to be the first on the scoreboard. Green Bay succeeded, toting up six points on two field goals kicked by Don Chandler. Then Starr completed a 62-yard touchdown pass to Boyd Dowler, and the Packers were up 13 to 0.

Raider quarterback Daryle Lamonica answered with a 23-yard touchdown pass to Bill Miller, and the extra point put the game at 13–7. They came close to a second touchdown before the half but had their hopes dashed when receiver Rodger Bird fumbled a catch that the Packers recovered. Starr worked his team into field goal range, and once again Don Chandler kicked the ball between the uprights for three.

With the score at 16–7 at the half, Lombardi delivered another locker room speech about how his team had to fight for the win. They did just that.

In the second half, the Packers' nine-point lead jumped to 16 when Starr passed to Max McGee for a 35-yard gain, and then made short passes to get the ball to the 2. From there, Donny Anderson pushed across the line for 6.

A fourth field goal later on put Green Bay up 26–7, but the final nail in the Raiders' coffin was a pass interception that was returned 60 yards for yet another touchdown. Although the Raiders managed to score the final touchdown of the game, it was too little too late. The final score was Packers 33, Raiders 14.

Two weeks later, Vince Lombardi resigned as Green Bay's coach. He stayed on as general manager through the 1968 season and then, finding he missed the thrill of coaching, accepted a position with the Washington Redskins. Under Lombardi the Redskins had a 7–5–2 season in 1969.

Unfortunately, no one will ever know how far he could have taken them. The hard-driving coach was diagnosed with cancer in mid-1970; he died on September 3, 1970. His legacy lives on each year, however; in 1971, the World Championship Trophy, awarded to the winning Super Bowl team, was renamed the Vince Lombardi Trophy in his honor.

⋆ CHAPTER THREE ⋆

1969

Broadway Joe

Throughout the 1960s, Vince Lombardi embodied the discipline that football demands. But toward the end of the decade, a new type of football star was emerging. Highly skilled, this new athlete was confident to the point of cockiness. No one personified that image more than the quarterback for the 1969 New York Jets, Joe Namath.

Joe Namath was young, good-looking, and outspoken. He joined the Jets in 1965 after a successful college career with the University of Alabama. At the end of his first season he was named AFL's Rookie of the Year; that same year saw him earn the nickname "Broadway Joe" for his celebrity lifestyle. In 1966 and 1967, he led the league in passing attempts, completions, and yards gained. In 1968 he helped the Jets to an 11–3 season, their first AFL championship, and a chance to play in Super Bowl III against the NFL's Baltimore Colts.

Few football followers expected Namath and the Jets to beat the Colts. Baltimore was coming off a 13–1 regular season and had just crushed the Cleveland Browns in a 34–0 defeat to take the NFL title. Even the picture on the game's program, in which a Colt player appears to be all but smothering a Jet player, suggested that the Colts were the stronger team.

But Broadway Joe believed otherwise. A few days before the game, he uttered a remark that has gone down in football history for its brazenness.

"The Jets will win on Sunday," he told reporters. "I guarantee it."

Namath's proclamation was boastful, but it was made with a purpose in mind. The Jets quarterback hoped to rattle the Colts, to make them angry enough that, come game day, they would make mistakes.

And Broadway Joe had another game-day strategy up his sleeve. He was known for his expert passing game, his ability to stay calm in the pocket, and to throw on the run. He knew that the Colts had studied films of his games and would know his strengths.

If they were smart, they'd be looking for him to play a passing game and would therefore cover his receivers like a second skin.

That's what Namath was counting on.

Super Bowl III was held on January 12, 1969, before a crowd that included President Richard Nixon and Vice President Spiro Agnew as well as comedians Bob Hope and Jackie Gleason. In three short years, the Super Bowl had gone from a less-than-packed house to the game famous and important people wanted to attend.

The Jets won the toss, but their first possession fizzled out.

The Colts began their drive from their own 27-yard line. Soon they were first-and-10 at the New York 19. A touchdown seemed inevitable, but the Colts just couldn't make it happen. First Willie Richardson dropped a pass. Then quarterback Earl Morrall overthrew a pass; on the next play, he was sacked. The Colts set up for a 27-yard field goal, but the kick went wide.

The game remained scoreless until close to the end of the first quarter. The Jets had possession on their own 17-yard line but lost the ball when a fumble was recovered by the Colts. The Baltimore team had only 12 yards to cover to get on the scoreboard.

Two plays later they still had 4 yards to go for a first down. Morrall faded back and rocketed a pass to linebacker Al Atkinson. Atkinson got a hand on the ball but couldn't make the catch. Instead, the ball rebounded off another Colt's shoulder and flew into the air.

Jets cornerback Randy Beverly dove for it, arms outstretched — and caught the ball in the end zone. Interception! The Jets had the ball on their own 20-yard line.

From there Namath started to work the ball down the field. He went to running back Matt Snell four plays in a row. Each time, Snell broke through the Colts' defense until the Jets had reached their own 46.

On the next play, the Colts blitzed. But Broadway Joe had anticipated their attack. Instead of being sacked, he got off a short pass to fullback Bill Mathis. Mathis caught it and the Jets were past the half-field mark for the first time in the game.

Four plays later they had pushed the Colts back to the 9-yard line. Namath got the ball to Snell for a gain of 5 more. Then it was Namath to Snell again — and before the Colts could stop them, the Jets had powered through for the first touchdown of the game. One kick later it was Jets 7, Colts 0.

While the Jets celebrated, the Colts stood by, stunned. The Jets had just run over them for an unbelievable 80-yard touchdown drive!

The Colts managed to get the ball deep into New York territory on the next possession. But then Morrall threw a pass that was intercepted by an ex-Colt named Johnny Sample.

"Here it is; here's what you're looking for," Sample taunted his old teammates.

Later, as the clock wound down toward halftime, the Colts got the ball to the Jets' 42. With less than a minute to go, Morrall called a "flea-flicker," an old-style play that moved the ball from the quarterback to a running back and back to the quarterback, who then looked for the receiver left open when the defense was drawn out of position.

True to the play, Morrall handed off to running back Tom Matte and then took off. Matte held the ball long enough for the defense to surge toward him. When they did, Matte lateralled the ball back to Morrall. Morrall looked for the open man.

Colt Jimmy Orr stood alone in the end zone. He waved his arms frantically, looking for the pass.

It never came, because Morrall couldn't see Orr. Why not? Football lore has it that Orr's blue-and-white uniform blended in with the blue-and-white uniforms of the team marching band that was then gathering behind the end zone!

Instead, Morrall threw to Jerry Hill. But the pass never made it to the intended receiver. Jets safety Jim Hudson stepped in front of Hill and grabbed the ball for the interception. Moments later, the halftime whistle blew.

In the locker room, Colts coach Don Shula lit into his players. "You've got them believing in themselves. You've got them believing that they're better than we are."

But in the end, it didn't matter what the Colts believed. The Jets were simply too pumped. Early in the third quarter, they turned a Colts fumble into a 32-yard field goal to put them up 10–0. Soon after, Earl Morrall was replaced by Johnny Unitas. But Unitas didn't fare any better than Morrall had.

Neither did the Colts' defense. Throughout the game, they had looked for Namath to go to the long pass. But Namath had injured his right thumb earlier, making such passes nearly impossible. The Colts didn't pick up on that fact and continued to drop back to cover receivers. And when they did, Broadway Joe responded by going to the short pass or running the ball. Soon the score was 13–0 in favor of the Jets.

Baltimore finally got on the scoreboard with a touchdown and extra point; but then, with less than two minutes left in the game, Namath moved the Jets into field-goal territory. One kick later, the score was 16–7 — and that's where it stayed.

Broadway Joe had backed up his brazen guarantee of a Jets win by bulling his team down the field and riding over the Colts to victory. Newspapers equated the upset to the biblical story of David defeating Goliath. They also made much of the fact that the victory was the first won by an AFL team. It was not to be the last, however — not by a long shot.

The following year marked the final days of the AFL-NFL competition. The merger of the two leagues had called for separate seasons through

1969, with the final interleague championship game, Super Bowl IV, to be played on January 11, 1970. When the AFL's Kansas City Chiefs bested the Minnesota Vikings 23–7 that game, the Super Bowl stood at two wins for the NFL and two for the AFL.

☆ CHAPTER FOUR ☆

1970–1974

Colts, Cowboys, Dolphins . . . and Dolphins

At the start of the 1970 season, the name AFL was dropped and the league officially became the NFL. The NFL consisted of 26 teams divided into two conferences, the National Football Conference (NFC) and the American Football Conference (AFC).

AFC teams played one another throughout the regular season, as did the NFC teams. At the end of the season, divisional playoff games were held; the winners then played one another for the conference title. And in January, the winner of the AFC title battled the winner of the NFC title in the Super Bowl.

In 1970, the Baltimore Colts were shifted to the AFC and went to their second Super Bowl to meet the Dallas Cowboys of the NFC. Early in the season few would have suspected that Dallas would be there, for after playing nine games, the Cowboys' record was only 5–4.

But Dallas roared back to win their last five games. Then they beat the Detroit Lions 5–0 for the division title and the San Francisco 49ers 17–10 to earn the right to face Baltimore.

The Colts wanted nothing more than to put the memories of the Super Bowl III loss away forever. "I still get flashbacks," Earl Morrall once admitted. "I've replayed in my mind that whole game over and over again. The interceptions, the flea-flicker, the whole mess."

Midway through the first quarter, however, things looked grim for the Colts. First, Dallas linebacker Chuck Howley made an interception that brought the ball to Baltimore's 46-yard line. The Colts' defense held and the Cowboys punted, but then the Colts' return man fumbled the ball! Dallas pounced on it at the Colts' 10-yard line. Suddenly the Cowboys were within striking distance of a touchdown.

The touchdown never came. The Colts' defense stayed tight, and Dallas walked away with a three-point field goal rather than a six-point touchdown.

Another field goal in the second quarter put the Cowboys up by six. The Colts needed a touchdown to tie the game.

They got it on a memorable and very controversial play.

It was third down and the Colts were stuck in their own territory. Quarterback Johnny Unitas took the snap and faded back, looking to pass. He saw receiver Eddie Hinton in the clear and threw. Too high! Hinton could only get a finger on it as it sailed overhead.

That finger tap sent the ball veering in a new direction, toward Cowboy Mel Renfro. Renfro leaped but couldn't grab the ball either.

The ball continued through the air, finally landing right into the hands of Colt John Mackey. Mackey barreled down the length of the field, a total of 75 yards, for a touchdown.

Yet even as Mackey was crossing into the end zone, the Cowboys were hollering that the touchdown didn't count. Back then, it was against the rules for two offensive players to touch the ball without a defensive player touching it in between. Renfro, the Cowboys claimed, hadn't touched the ball.

The officials huddled up to discuss the situation. When they broke apart, they ruled that Renfro had in fact touched the ball. The touchdown stayed on the scoreboard.

When film of that moment was reviewed later, it was obvious that Renfro's fingernail had grazed the ball and that the officials had made the right call. But with the Super Bowl on the line, plenty of Cowboy fans and players felt they had been robbed. They were somewhat mollified when the team blocked the Colts' extra-point attempt to keep the score tied at 6–6.

So far, with an interception, a fumble after a punt, and the controversy over Mackey's touchdown, Super Bowl V had been anything but pretty. It got even uglier as the play continued.

First, Unitas fumbled while trying to run the ball. Dallas recovered on Baltimore's 28 and moments later scored their first touchdown. The extra point was good, giving Dallas a 13–6 lead. Soon after, Unitas got clobbered when a defensive end tackled him in mid-throw. Unitas's pass went for his second interception — and Unitas went to the sidelines with bruised ribs.

Earl Morrall came in at quarterback for the Colts. With a combination of long passes, he brought Baltimore to the Dallas 2. Unfortunately, that's where they stayed. The Cowboy defense was just too tight for the Colts to bull a man across the line. At halftime, the score remained Cowboys 13, Colts 6.

Baltimore's troubles continued in the second half when return man Jim Duncan fumbled the opening kickoff. Dallas hoped to convert his mistake into another touchdown, but six plays later Cowboy Duane Thomas lost the ball. There was a mad scramble for the loose ball that ended with Duncan recovering. That possession didn't yield a touchdown either. Going into the final quarter, the score was still 13–6.

With the clock ticking down, Morrall called the same play that had been the Colts' downfall two years earlier — the flea-flicker. This time, he chucked the ball to running back Sam Havrilak. According to the play, Havrilak was then supposed to lateral the ball back to Morrall. But the running back saw a defensive man hurtling in toward Morrall, so he dished the ball to John Mackey instead.

The ball never reached Mackey. Baltimore's Eddie Hinton had grabbed it and was making for the end zone.

Dallas's Cornell Green gave chase and flattened Hinton, knocking the ball free. Six players grabbed for it as it bounced into and out of the end zone. Finally, the referee ruled a touchback. Dallas had the ball at their own 20-yard line.

More mayhem followed when Dallas turned over the ball on a tipped pass that landed in the hands of a Colt. That player brought it to the Cowboy 3-yard line. Moments later, the Colts blasted into the end zone for their first touchdown. The extra point tied the game at 13 apiece.

The score stayed tied until the last minute of the game. As the clock ticked down, Baltimore gained possession on Dallas's 28-yard line. They tried but failed to get a first down.

Rookie Colts kicker Jim O'Brien hustled in from the bench for the field goal attempt. It was the most important moment of his young career. If he made it, he'd be a hero. If he failed, the game would go into overtime.

The ball was snapped and placed. O'Brien drew

back his leg and kicked. The ball soared through the air and between the uprights! With a mere five seconds remaining on the clock, Baltimore took the game, 16–13.

O'Brien leaped into the air. The Colts went wild. Thanks to O'Brien's kick, their 1968 loss was finally behind them.

Dallas fans were bitterly disappointed at the Super Bowl V loss. But to their delight, the Cowboys put together another stellar season in 1971 and once again made it to the Super Bowl. On January 16, 1972, the Super Bowl V losers met the Miami Dolphins.

Coached by Don Shula, the Dolphins were a strong team. But the Cowboys were even stronger. Dallas quarterback Roger "the Dodger" Staubach led the charge, receivers Mike Ditka and Lance Alworth provided steady hands, and the team's "Doomsday Defense" allowed Miami to gain just 185 yards, a Super Bowl record that still stands. In the end, the Cowboys rode circles around the floundering Dolphins, chalking up 24 points with a field goal in the first period, and then a touchdown in each of the quarters that followed. Miami, on the other hand, managed only one measly field goal.

In the end, however, it was the Miami Dolphins who got the last laugh. A year after their Super Bowl VI defeat, they returned to the championship game again, riding high on a perfect record of 14–0 plus two post-season wins. The Cowboys, meanwhile, were left behind after a loss to the Washington Redskins in the NFC title game.

The Redskins hardly seemed like Super Bowl contenders. Quarterback Billy Kilmer had an unpredictable arm and often flubbed passes when under pressure. The team's best halfback, Larry Brown, was capable of bulling his way through tough defensive coverage, but even he had trouble when the defense targeted him.

Don Shula took advantage of the Redskins' weaknesses. He instructed his front line to focus their full attention on Kilmer and Brown, and then sat back and waited for Washington to fall beneath Miami's might.

And fall they did, although not quite as hard as some had suspected they would. The Dolphins' offense racked up two touchdowns in the first half, and their defense allowed the Redskins to cross the midfield line only once.

The Redskins got on the board in the second half, however, following a blocked Dolphin field goal attempt that found the ball bouncing back into the hands of the startled Dolphin kicker, Garo Yepremian. Yepremian did what most people faced with a sea of rushing football players would do: he got rid of the ball. Unfortunately for the Dolphins, the throw was picked off by Redskin Mike Bass, who then barreled into the Dolphin end zone.

But for Washington, the most exciting — and ultimately disappointing — moment of the game came right at the end. With two minutes left on the clock, the Dolphins were forced to punt. The Redskins had a last-minute chance to tie the game.

They couldn't do it. Kilmer's first two passes were incomplete. On the next play, his handoff to Brown was successful, but Brown was pushed back for a 4-yard loss. With the game on the line and 14 yards to go, Kilmer had no choice but to try a long bomb. But the ball never left his hands. He was sacked on the play, and the Dolphins made history by completing the first perfect NFL season ever.

Miami followed that Super Bowl victory with a second one the following year, besting the Minnesota Vikings 24–7 on January 13, 1974. It was the Dolphins' third consecutive trip to the Super Bowl, another first in NFL history. That win marked the end of the Dolphin era, however, for there was a new AFC team on the rise.

★ CHAPTER FIVE ★

1975–1976

The Steelers Steal the Show

At the end of the 1974 season, the Pittsburgh Steelers emerged as the powerhouse of the AFC. The team boasted many future Hall-of-Famers, including quarterback Terry Bradshaw, defensive tackle "Mean Joe" Greene, and Franco Harris, whose famous "Immaculate Reception" during the division playoff game on December 23, 1973, had given the Steelers their first post-season victory. Together, they and the rest of the team executed Chuck Noll's coaching strategy to a 12–3–1 post-season record and their first shot at the Vince Lombardi Trophy.

The Steelers' competition was the Minnesota Vikings, two-time losers in previous Super Bowls. The Vikings had high hopes that their third trip would yield a victory — and they had good reason to believe they would see their hopes realized. Their quarterback, Fran Tarkenton, was one of the best scramblers in the NFL and had led the NFC with 2,598 passing yards that season. Their Vikings' offense was strong, scoring more than 300 points in their 10 regular-season wins. Their defense was even stronger, having given up less than 200 points overall.

Both teams came out strong defensively; and, try as they might, neither Tarkenton nor Bradshaw could move the ball very far into the other team's territory. The only points scored in the first half came when Tarkenton muffed a pitchout to Dave Osborn. Osborn fumbled but managed to fall on the ball. Unfortunately, he fell on it in Pittsburgh's end zone. The officials ruled a safety and awarded the Steelers two points.

The Vikings suffered another bad break in the opening minutes of the second half. The Steelers kicked off. Viking Bill Brown caught the ball and ran 4 yards. That's as far as he got. Suddenly the ball squirted out of his hands. Fumble!

Steeler Marv Kellum pounced on it at Minnesota's 30-yard line. Franco Harris took command, running the ball 24 yards closer to the end zone. Then, after a loss of three, he swept around the defense and charged the final 9 yards for the game's first touchdown. The Steelers led, 9–0.

But the Vikings weren't beaten yet. They drew within three of Pittsburgh in the fourth quarter on a blocked punt that was recovered for a Minnesota touchdown. Unfortunately for Viking fans, the extra point was no good.

With ten minutes left in the game, the score stood at 9–6. Then Terry Bradshaw started a drive down the field, from the Pittsburgh 34 all the way to the Minnesota 4. On the next play, he rolled out, saw Brown in the end zone, and launched a fireball into his hands. The Vikings couldn't respond, and when the game ended, the Steelers had clinched their first Super Bowl, 16–6.

The Steelers went into the next season full of confidence after their Super Bowl victory. They romped through the schedule to a 12–2 record and blasted by their competition in the post-season to earn their second trip to the Super Bowl.

Their opponents were the winners of Super Bowl VI, the Dallas Cowboys. With Roger Staubach as the quarterback, the one-time champs had battled their way to a ten and four season. In the postseason they beat the Vikings and the Los Angeles Rams to take their place in the Super Bowl for the third time.

Both teams were hungry for a win. The Steelers wanted to defend their title as world champs, and the Cowboys were looking to make their Super Bowl record 2–1 instead of 1–2.

Many football followers thought the Steelers would prove too powerful for the Cowboys. And at first that seemed true. Harris plowed through the Dallas defense, carrying the ball four times in five plays. But it was the Cowboys who got on the board first, turning a fumbled punt snap into a touchdown.

Pittsburgh answered with seven points of its own thanks to a 32-yard bomb from Bradshaw to Lynn Swann followed by a 7-yard pass into the end zone that, combined with the extra point, tied up the game.

Dallas broke the tie with a field goal, and the score stayed 10–7 through the third quarter. Then the Steelers added two to their side with a safety after a blocked punt. Pittsburgh took its first lead of the game soon after on a 36-yard field goal. They got three more after intercepting a Staubach pass.

The score was now 15–10 in favor of Pittsburgh. But there was still time on the clock, and the Cowboys knew that they could take the game if they could get just one more touchdown.

But when that touchdown finally came, it was too little, too late, because the Steelers had already chalked up an additional 6 points of their own.

The winning touchdown came two seconds shy of the twelfth minute of the 4th quarter. Bradshaw saw a blitz coming. Knowing that that defensive power play meant fewer men were on his receivers, he looked for someone to pass to. Lynn Swann was covered by just one man. Bradshaw unleashed a long bomb 59 yards into Swann's waiting hands, and Swann danced into the Cowboys' end zone. Bradshaw, meanwhile, lay unconscious after a punishing tackle.

Swann's touchdown catch was his fourth of the day, a total of 161 yards. "It always makes me feel good when our passing game plays such a big part in a victory," Swann said after the game.

Swann was named MVP. His performance was remarkable in and of itself, but even more so because only days before the game, he had been lying in a hospital recovering from a concussion. Doctors had warned him that if he sustained another bad blow to the head during the Super Bowl, he might suffer permanent brain damage. Swann decided it was worth the risk. His efforts that day helped his team to their second consecutive Super Bowl win.

★ CHAPTER SIX ★

1977–1980

Steelers Again!

With each passing season, the rivalry between the AFC and the NFC grew ever fiercer, ensuring that the Super Bowl would continue to be the most-watched sporting event each year. Super Bowl XI saw the Oakland Raiders winning their first Lombardi Trophy, leaving the Minnesota Vikings out in the cold for the fourth time in eight years. Super Bowl XII matched the Denver Broncos against the Dallas Cowboys. The Broncos had a miserable game with four fumbles, all of which were recovered by Dallas, and four interceptions, two of which yielded points for the opposition. The Cowboys won that game 27–10.

Super Bowl XIII was a rematch between the Cowboys and the Steelers. Dallas had a Super Bowl record of 2 wins, 2 losses. Pittsburgh had two wins to its credit but no losses. Whoever won this game would make history as the first team to win three Super Bowls.

To the casual observer, the Steelers were the better team. Their offense was fantastic. Terry Bradshaw had thrown 28 touchdowns in 1979, 20 of those to either Lynn Swann or John Stallworth. Franco Harris and Rocky Bleier had a combined average of one touchdown per game. And the defense did its part, too, holding the opposition to less than 200 points that year.

Meanwhile, the Cowboys had struggled in the beginning of their season, winning only six of their first ten games. Then Roger Staubach and the rest of the team had pulled it together and won their last eight. Now, they were just as eager as the Steelers to grab their spot in NFL history.

With a third Super Bowl win on the line, people anticipated that this game was going to be one of the best yet. They were not disappointed.

The Cowboys threatened early on in the first quarter with a drive that found them on the Pittsburgh 35-yard line. But they flubbed a double reverse play, and the Steelers recovered at their own

47. Six plays later, Pittsburgh stood at the Dallas 28. On the next snap, Bradshaw found Stallworth in the end zone for the game's first score. The extra point put the Steelers up 7–0.

The Steelers kept the Cowboys from crossing the midfield line until the last minute of the first quarter. Then, with Pittsburgh in possession, Dallas sacked Bradshaw. Bradshaw fumbled, and Dallas recovered on the Pittsburgh 41. Three plays later, Staubach blasted a pass to Tony Hill at the 26-yard line. Hill dashed down the sideline and into the end zone to tie the score.

The first five minutes of the second quarter yielded two more touchdowns, one for each team. Then, with the score knotted at 14–14, Staubach threw his only interception.

The Steelers used the turnover to motor down the gridiron. With 33 seconds left in the half, Bradshaw lofted a pass to Bleier in the end zone. The Steelers were ahead for the first time in the game.

"Of all the passes I've ever made," Staubach said of the interception-turned-touchdown, "this one will haunt me the longest."

But it was Staubach's teammate, Jackie Smith,

who wound up as the real goat of the game. Smith was a veteran player known for his steady hands. He'd come out of retirement to play for the Cowboys that year. This was his first Super Bowl.

It was third-and-three on Pittsburgh's 10. Staubach took the snap and looked for the open man. Smith stood alone in the end zone. Staubach shot him a pass. Smith reached out, caught the ball — and then dropped it.

"That wasn't exactly the way we had worked on it," Smith said ruefully. "I lost my footing, my feet ended up in front of me, and I think the ball went off my hip. I've dropped passes before, but never any that was so important."

Staubach refused to let Smith take all the heat, saying, "if you're casting blame, it's 50 percent my fault and 50 percent Jackie's." Still, history remembers Smith's dropped catch as making the difference in the game. The Cowboys wound up with a 3-point field goal rather than a 7-point, game-tying touchdown.

But it was in the fourth quarter that the most controversial play in Super Bowl history occurred. The Steelers had possession on the Dallas 44. Bradshaw got off a short pass toward Lynn Swann. The ball never reached him.

Covering Swann was Dallas cornerback Benny Barnes. One moment, Swann was reaching for the pass. The next, he and Barnes were tangled up in a heap on the ground and the ball was bouncing free. But who had tripped whom?

According to one source, it was Swann who tripped Barnes. "Swann ran right up my back," Barnes himself recalled. An official who had an unobstructed view of the play apparently agreed, for he didn't call Barnes for tripping.

But on another side of the field, a second official saw Barnes's feet fly up and catch Swann. He threw a flag, calling a tripping violation. Despite heated arguments from the Cowboys' bench, the ruling stayed and the ball was returned to the line of scrimmage. Three plays later, Franco Harris tore across the goal line for a touchdown to put the Steelers up by 11. When the Cowboys fumbled the kickoff, the Steelers added another seven.

But the Cowboys weren't done yet. With less than three minutes left on the clock, Staubach marched his squad 89 yards for a touchdown to put the game at 35–24. Then the Steelers muffed the kickoff return, and suddenly the Cowboys had tallied up another seven.

The Cowboys had surged back to make the score 35–31, but that's as good as it got for them. The clock wound down, and Pittsburgh had its third Super Bowl victory. Terry Bradshaw was named MVP, having thrown for 318 yards — a Super Bowl record — and four touchdowns.

Bradshaw's comment after the game was typical of the plain-spoken, fun-loving Louisiana native: "This sure was a lot of fun!"

The fun continued for Pittsburgh the following year when they made yet another trip to the Super Bowl. It was the second time they had made back-to-back journeys to the big game; if they won, they would be the only team to ever take consecutive Super Bowls twice, and the only one to win four Super Bowls.

Their opponents were the Los Angeles Rams. Up until that season, the Rams had been a consistently strong team but had never made it to the Super Bowl. In 1979, they had their worst season in years, going only 9–7. However, this was the year they blasted past the competition in the post-season to go to the Super Bowl.

The game was played on January 20, 1980. The Steelers got off to a quick start with a 41-yard field goal on their first possession. But the Rams answered with a touchdown that took them only eight plays to make. The score seesawed back in favor of the Steelers in the next period following a 1-yard touchdown run by Franco Harris. Back it went again to the Rams when two field goals gave them six more points before the end of the half.

Three minutes into the third quarter, the Rams' 13–10 lead was swallowed by the Steelers when Bradshaw bombed a 47-yard pass to Lynn Swann in the end zone.

After the kick, Los Angeles moved the length of the field in four plays thanks in large part to a 50-yard pass from quarterback Vince Ferragamo to Billy Waddy that put them on Pittsburgh's 24. Then came a 22-yard touchdown pass from an unlikely thrower, halfback Lawrence McCutcheon, to wide receiver Ron Smith. The extra point was no good, but still the Rams were up 19–17.

They held that lead longer than expected when Bradshaw threw not one but two interceptions. "I was so dad-blame mad at that [second] interception I couldn't see straight," Bradshaw commented later.

The Steelers' quarterback redeemed himself early in the last quarter, however. The ball was on Pittsburgh's 27-yard line. It was third down with 8 yards to go. Bradshaw took the snap and faded back. Meanwhile, receiver John Stallworth hustled 15 yards down the field and then hooked away from the defensive men covering him. As Stallworth ran deep, Bradshaw fired off a perfect spiral pass that went an amazing 73 yards, was nearly picked off by a Los Angeles defender, but instead landed in Stallworth's arms at the Rams' 39. Stallworth charged the rest of the way to put the Steelers up 24–19.

The Rams never recovered. Ferragamo threw an interception, and the Steelers scored again with less than two minutes on the clock. With a final score of 31–19, the Steelers had made Super Bowl history. Bradshaw was named Most Valuable Player for the second year in a row, an award that pleased him as much as it surprised him.

"They seldom give such honors to quarterbacks who throw three interceptions," the future Hall of Famer and sportscaster joked.

The Pittsburgh Steelers were undoubtedly the most dominant team of the 1970s. But after their fourth Super Bowl title in 1980, their star faded. They would not return to the big game for 16 years. And in the meantime, other teams and other stars were on the rise.

⋆ CHAPTER SEVEN ⋆

1981–1986

Rising Quarterbacks and
Super-Powered Defenses

In 1981, Super Bowl XV was played between the Oakland Raiders and the Philadelphia Eagles. It was Philadelphia's first trip to the game and Oakland's third. The Raiders' last trip had been their 1977 win over Minnesota; previously, they had lost to the Green Bay Packers in 1968. They were determined to break their 1–1 record with another win. They got their wish, defeating the Eagles 27–10.

The next year saw two different teams, the San Francisco 49ers and the Cincinnati Bengals, making their maiden voyages to the Super Bowl. That either team was there at all was somewhat remarkable. The Bengals had been in the cellar just one year before, and the 49ers had suffered through six losing seasons in a row.

But both teams had undergone a significant

turnaround in the 1981 season. The Bengals put together a 14–2 record behind the quarterback talent of Ken Anderson. With twenty-five-year-old Joe Montana at the helm for their team, the 49ers won 13 of their 16 regular season games.

The two teams took to the field under the Pontiac Silverdome in Michigan on January 24, the first Super Bowl to take place in the north. The 49ers elected to receive but immediately lost possession when the return was fumbled on the Bengals' 26. Fortunately for the 49ers, Anderson gave them back the ball when he threw an interception instead of a touchdown.

Joe Montana took control after that, first by marching his team 68 yards down the field and then by diving 1 yard into the end zone to put San Francisco on the board. In the second quarter, he turned a Bengal fumble into a 49er touchdown, working his team 92 yards in 12 plays. A field goal 18 seconds before the half put San Francisco up 17–0.

That's how the score should have stayed going into the locker room, but instead, the Bengals flubbed the kickoff return. A 49er pounced on it at Cincinnati's 4-yard line, and San Francisco added three more points to their side with a field goal. Thanks to Bengal errors, they were up by 20 points.

But the Bengals came back after halftime with their claws sharpened and their teeth bared. Anderson answered Montana's earlier touchdown dive with a 5-yard TD plunge of his own. Midway through the fourth quarter Cincinnati got on the board again to draw within six.

Meanwhile, Cincinnati's defense tightened around San Francisco. The 49ers didn't reach the end zone again, although they did sweeten their lead with two more field goals. The Bengals managed to add another touchdown, but it wasn't enough to give them the win. The final score read San Francisco 26, Cincinnati 21.

The 49ers now had two Super Bowl wins under their belt, and many expected they would rise to the top again the following year. They didn't. In a season that was abbreviated to nine games due to a player strike, San Francisco won only three times. That year's Super Bowl went to the Washington Redskins, who beat the Miami Dolphins 27–17.

The Redskins returned to the limelight again the following year, this time facing the recently relocated

Los Angeles Raiders. The Raiders got on the board early, turning a blocked punt into a touchdown. Soon after, L.A. quarterback Jim Plunkett sent the ball into the arms of Cliff Branch for a 50-yard gain. Two plays later, the Raiders had netted seven more points. With the score 14–0 the Redskins finally put the ball through the uprights for a field goal. There were only a few minutes left before the half at that point, and most expected the score going into half-time would stay 14–3. But it didn't.

With 12 seconds left on the clock, the Redskins took possession at their own 12-yard line. Most teams in this position would choose to run out the clock or throw a long pass far downfield, out of harm's way. Instead, Redskin quarterback Joe Theis-man readied his team for a short screen pass. The play called for three linesmen to cover the quarter-back on the right while he threw a pass to a receiver on the left. A similar play had fooled the Raiders earlier in the season.

This time, however, the play backfired. The Raiders' coach recognized the setup and quickly sent in his tallest linebacker, Jack Squirek, with in-structions to get between the Redskins receiver Joe

Washington and the ball. As hoped, when Theisman unleashed a pass to Washington, Squirek was ready. He intercepted Theisman's throw and ran it into the end zone for a touchdown seven seconds before the clock ran out.

Early in the second half, the Redskins rebounded with a touchdown on their opening drive. But those six points — the extra-point kick was blocked — were the only additional ones they would gain. Los Angeles, on the other hand, drove through for two more touchdowns as well as a field goal to make the final score a crushing 38–9.

The 1984 season saw the return to power of the San Francisco 49ers. Joe Montana had a fantastic year, throwing and passing for nearly 3,000 yards to his go-to men, fullback Roger Craig and running back Wendell Tyler. They reached the Super Bowl easily with a regular season record of 15 wins, an NFL record at the time.

Their opponents were the powerful Miami Dolphins. The Dolphins were coming off their second winning season in a row, thanks in large part to their new superstar quarterback, Dan Marino. In 1984, Marino threw for over 5,000 yards and 48 touchdowns. His accuracy and strength were fearsome, and his offensive line was just as intimidating.

With two such incredible quarterbacks pitted against each other, many expected Super Bowl XIX to be one of the highest-scoring matches yet. And in the first half, it seemed those expectations would be met.

The Dolphins struck first with a 33-yard field goal for three. Then the 49ers gained seven after a 33-yard pass from Montana to running back Carl Monroe. The Dolphins took the lead again with a touchdown of their own to make it 10–7.

San Francisco turned the tables in the second quarter. They had realized that Miami's left-side defense was being mowed down by San Francisco's hefty tackle, Bubba Paris, time and again. Montana exploited this weakness to gain critical yards and keep possession of the ball.

The Dolphins, meanwhile, were beginning to have problems. First their kicker flubbed several punts, giving the 49ers prime position on the field. San Francisco pressed their advantage, scoring three touchdowns in as many possessions. Miami answered with two field goals before the end of the half to draw within 12, but those six points were the last they would add to their score. The 49ers rode over them for much of the second half, chalking up another field goal and a final touchdown in the third quarter. Their defense rattled Marino; and with a 38–16 lead, San Francisco simply had to keep Miami from scoring — and as the clock finally ran out, that's just what they did.

The 49ers now owned two Super Bowl rings, and they wanted more. They had a few years to wait for them, however. In 1986, it was the Chicago Bears who took center stage.

The Bears had never been to the Super Bowl before, but this year no one had any doubt that they deserved their spot. Their defensive might, including the immovable force of 350-pound rookie William "The Refrigerator" Perry and the superb play of Mike Singletary, was astonishing. The secondary seemed to have a sixth sense for where the ball would be thrown and nabbed 23 interceptions. Their offense, led by quarterback Jim McMahon and aided by Walter "Sweetness" Payton, scored more points than any other team in the NFC that season.

They certainly scored more points than their opponents in Super Bowl XX. The New England Patriots were also making their first trip to the game; but, unlike Chicago, they seemed far out of their league. Although they scored first with a field goal after a fumble by Payton, after that, the points quickly mounted up in favor of the Bears: from 3–0 it became 3–3, then 6–3, 13–3, 20–3, and 23–3 — all before halftime! Chicago posted an amazing 236 yards for the first half. New England, on the other hand, was in negative numbers with minus 19 yards, and had only made one first down and two pass completions to boot.

The second half was a romp in the park for the Bears. At times, they seemed to be taunting the Patriots. One touchdown play found the Fridge in a three-point stance behind McMahon. Obviously, the ball would be handed to him — yet, even though they were expecting it, New England couldn't stop the massive Bear from flattening them on his way into the end zone.

Chicago's final score of 46 points was the highest any team had ever scored in a Super Bowl to date. While Bears fans were overjoyed at their team's de-

Vince Lombardi, legendary coach of the Green Bay Packers and the man for whom the Super Bowl Trophy is named, watches as his team wins the AFL-NFL Championship Game in 1967.

"Broadway Joe" Namath watches as his pass reaches the hands of the intended receiver in the Jets-Colts Super Bowl III upset of 1969.

Quarterback Terry Bradshaw is all smiles after leading the Pittsburgh Steelers to victory in Super Bowl XIII. The 1979 win was the third championship title for the team.

Cowboy Jackie Smith is the face of defeat. He dropped a game-winning touchdown pass from Roger Staubach in Super Bowl XIII.

After suffering three Super Bowl defeats, John Elway and the Broncos won back-to-back championships in 1998 and 1999. Here, Elway bulls across the line to help his team to their second consecutive victory.

Yes! San Francisco 49er Joe Montana flings his arms skyward after completing a pass to receiver Jerry Rice in Super Bowl XXIV. The 49ers annihilated the Denver Broncos, 55–10, the widest margin of any Super Bowl.

Kevin Dyson of the Tennessee Titans gives it his all, but Ram Mike Jones makes sure he falls just inches short of the goal line in Super Bowl XXXIV.

The Patriots beat the Philadelphia Eagles 24–21 in Super Bowl XXXIX, thanks to a last-second field goal kicked by Adam Vinatieri, held aloft here just moments after giving his team their third Super Bowl victory in four years.

cisive victory, many people felt that the mismatch had taken the "Super" out of the Super Bowl game. They longed for the excitement that equally matched teams generated and wondered if they would see it again the following year — or if Super Bowl XXI would be another case of one team running roughshod over the other.

✶ CHAPTER EIGHT ✶

1987–1988

Bucking the Broncos

Most people assumed the mighty Bears would reach the Super Bowl again in 1987. But instead, Chicago was defeated in the NFC championship game by the Washington Redskins. Many people also assumed that the 49ers were bound for another trip, but that team was upset even before reaching the AFC title game.

Instead, the two teams that met in 1987 were the New York Giants and the Denver Broncos. It was a sweet moment for the Giants, a team that had struggled to reach that spot for more than two decades. Phil Simms, the quarterback, had struggled too; for eight years, Giants fans had considered him subpar. Now, at last, he had a chance to prove just what he was capable of.

Simms's counterpart for the Broncos, John Elway,

was just as eager to show his stuff. Elway and Simms had very different quarterbacking styles. Where Simms was cautious, Elway was daring. Simms relied on the crushing talent of his star linebacker, Lawrence "LT" Taylor to clear the way for him. Elway also had a strong defense that bought him time, but the Broncos quarterback wasn't afraid to use a little razzle-dazzle to make a play work.

At the start of Super Bowl XXI, Elway razzle-dazzled his team close to a touchdown but had to settle for a field goal instead.

On his first possession, Simms drove all the way into the end zone with six straight and accurate passes. Elway came right back, moving the ball down the field 58 yards to put seven more points on their side of the board. The Broncos threatened again soon after, but this time, New York's defense was so tight Denver couldn't get across the line. Nor could their kicker put the ball through the uprights on the field goal attempt.

The score stayed 10–7 Broncos until late in the second quarter, when the Giants defense sacked Elway in Denver's end zone for a two-point safety. After the kickoff, the Broncos pushed them down the field to come within field-goal range. But once again, their kicker missed. The score going into halftime was 10–9 in favor of the Broncos.

It didn't stay that way for long. Early in the second half, the Giants had possession but couldn't make it past the midfield line. Then, on fourth down, they tried a fake punt. It worked, gaining them the 2 yards they needed. Simms then finessed the team down the field and into the end zone to give the Giants their first lead. They added another three on a field goal to make it Giants 19, Broncos 10.

Simms was successfully picking apart the Broncos defense. In the third quarter, he and running back Joe Morris worked the old flea-flicker play. Simms handed off to Morris. Morris pitched back to Simms, who then hurled the ball long to receiver Phil McConkey. McConkey nabbed it at the 10 and ran to the 1. Moments later, he was in the end zone for six more points. The extra kick made it New York 26, Denver 10.

The Broncos did their best to buck off the Giants' defense, but to little avail. Although Denver's kicker finally succeeded in putting the ball between the uprights for a field goal and the team bulled into the end zone for a touchdown, Simms and the Giants chalked up 13 more points for a final score of Giants 39, Broncos 20.

Phil Simms had had a record-setting game. He'd thrown 22 completions in 25 attempts, an amazing 88 completion percentage for a total of 268 yards. Of those 22, 10 were in a row, the greatest number of consecutive completions in any Super Bowl yet. His throws had netted three touchdowns and, even more impressive, he hadn't thrown a single interception despite facing one of the toughest defenses in the league.

His coach, Bill Parcells, summed up Simms's feat in simple terms: "This might be the best game a quarterback has ever played."

Simms's Super Bowl performance would prove to be a tough act to follow. But the next year, a new quarterback emerged who did more than play a terrific game — he busted apart a stereotype that had long plagued professional football, namely, that players of African-American heritage were not smart enough to play quarterback.

Doug Williams of the Washington Redskins was an unlikely hero. Two years before joining the

Redskins as backup quarterback he had been out of work, left high and dry when the ill-fated United States Football League (USFL) folded in 1985. Prior to the USFL he had played for the Tampa Bay Buccaneers; but even though Williams had years of experience, few people believed he would be the Redskins' answer for a topnotch quarterback.

Williams took over for the Redskins' starting quarterback, Jay Schroeder, midway through the 1987 season. While Williams was consistent, his plays were low-key rather than inspiring. Still, he helped the team win in the playoffs to earn its fourth trip to the Super Bowl.

Williams's competition in the big game was the hugely popular John Elway. Despite his team's loss in the previous Super Bowl, Elway's star had continued to grow brighter throughout the 1987 season. His talent was a major reason the Broncos had reached the Super Bowl for the second straight year. Compared to Elway, many people thought Williams lacked the spark that made good quarterbacks great.

In the days leading up to the game, reporters made a big to-do about Williams's race. He was football's Jackie Robinson, they claimed, breaking the football color barrier just as Robinson had broken baseball's 40 years earlier.

"I'm no Jackie Robinson," Williams responded when he heard such talk. And in some ways, that was true. He wasn't the only black football player, or even the only black quarterback in the league. However, he was the first black quarterback in the Super Bowl — and that made him a topic of much discussion.

But on Super Bowl Sunday 1988, any talk about the color of Williams's skin soon turned to talk about his unexpected and thrilling play.

The Broncos were the heavy favorites that day; and, true to form, they got on the board first when Elway launched a 56-yard touchdown pass two minutes into the game. They followed those seven points with a three-point field goal to go up 10–0.

The Redskins, meanwhile, were playing as if they believed that they were the lesser team. Their problems mounted when Williams was benched with a twisted knee in the first quarter.

Yet Williams himself didn't seem rattled. He re-entered the game in the second quarter — and never looked back. On the Redskins' first possession, he took the snap at Washington's 20-yard line and looked to make a short pass to wideout Ricky Sanders. The play appeared to have been broken up when Sanders was shoved aside. But Sanders didn't stop moving. Instead, he charged downfield. Williams saw him in the clear and fired off a perfect pass. Sanders gathered it in and ran the rest of the way into the end zone. Suddenly, the Redskins were behind by only three.

And, just as suddenly, they jumped ahead by four. The touchdown came when the intended receiver was moved off course and went long, and Williams connected for a touchdown pass.

The Broncos looked to tighten things up with a field goal. But as in the previous Super Bowl, their kicker couldn't find the space between the uprights. The Redskins reclaimed the ball and promptly ran it 58 yards for their third touchdown of the quarter. With the score now at 21–10, Denver suddenly seemed the weaker team.

Williams pressed the advantage to throw yet another touchdown pass, this one a 50-yard bomb, to put the Redskins up by an amazing 18 points. And they weren't done yet! After John Elway panicked in the pocket and threw an interception, Williams made Super Bowl history by spiraling his fifth touchdown of the period.

Going into the second half, the Broncos were down 35 to 10 — and things got worse. Elway was sacked five times, destroying Denver's chances of launching a comeback. And when the Redskins scored yet another touchdown to make the final score 42–10, the disheartened Broncos were finished.

Not surprisingly, Doug Williams was named Super Bowl XXII's best player. Coach Joe Gibbs was full of admiration for his team and especially for the unemployed quarterback whose career he had resurrected. "Maybe now," he said, "they will look at Doug for something other than his color."

⋆ CHAPTER NINE ⋆

1989–1990

Return of the 49ers

Super Bowl XXII had featured one of the greatest second quarters ever played. But for some, the game was a yawner because the outcome had been so obvious by halftime. Those fans wished for the last-minute upsets and come-from-behind victories that made football so exciting to watch.

They got their wish the following year. Super Bowl XXIII, between the San Francisco 49ers and the Cincinnati Bengals, went right down to the wire.

The Bengals had put together a fantastic season in 1988, winning all eight of their home games and going four-for-four on the road — quite an achievement for the team that had had the worst record in the AFC the previous year! Their turnaround had been in large part due to their quarterback, Boomer

Esiason, who in 1988 led the conference with 28 touchdowns.

The 49ers had their star quarterback, Joe Montana, and their equally strong backup QB, Steve Young. The 49ers also had the best pass catcher in the league, Jerry Rice.

The game promised to be a tough battle, but no one expected it to be bloody. Yet by the end of the first quarter, San Francisco's Steve Wallace was out with a broken ankle and Tim Krumrie of the Bengals had had his leg shattered in three places. Alongside these injuries, the three-point field goal by the 49ers seemed almost an afterthought.

The game ground down into a defensive struggle in the second quarter. Neither team could move the ball far enough into the other's territory to score a touchdown, although a few minutes before the half, the Bengals managed to tie it up with a field goal.

The offense continued to slumber in the third quarter. On the opening possession, Esiason marched his men down the field only to see their touchdown hopes turn into yet another field goal. They didn't hold their three-point lead for long, however. Esiason threw an interception that the 49ers returned for another field goal.

With the score knotted at 6 apiece and the third quarter ticking to a close, San Francisco kicked off. Stanford Jennings of the Bengals caught the ball on the 7 and began to run. He passed the 10, the 15, the 20 — and all the other hash marks on the field as he dodged and weaved his way into the end zone, a 93-yard return!

The 49ers were stunned, but they didn't despair. Instead, they came back fighting with a sweet three-play drive that ended with Montana connecting with Rice in the end zone. Once again, the game was tied.

Then disaster struck the 49ers. They had the go-ahead points lined up with a field goal — but their kicker missed the attempt. The Bengals made sure they didn't follow suit. On their next drive, they sent the ball soaring through the uprights to make it 16–13 with less than three minutes left.

But as the saying goes, it ain't over until it's over — and for San Francisco, it wasn't over, not by a long shot. After the kickoff, Montana worked his team down the field one short pass at a time. Five plays later they were near the 50-yard line. Two plays more put them at the Bengals' 35.

Then Cincinnati got lucky. A 49er was flagged on a play, and San Francisco was forced to move back to the 45. The 49ers were out of field-goal range, and the clock was still ticking down.

San Francisco decided to go for broke. On the next play, Montana found Rice, who bolted down the sideline to the 18. From there, they pushed to the 10.

There were 39 seconds left on the clock. Montana consulted with his coach, and they agreed on a play called the "20 Halfback Curl X-Up." The play called for three receivers to race into the end zone. When faced with similar situations in the past, the Bengals had chosen to double-team two of those receivers and cover the third with one man. Montana was counting on them to do the same thing again. If they did, then the two double-teamed receivers would rush for the corners, drawing their men with them and leaving the middle ground open. The third receiver would make for that middle ground. If all went well, he would outdistance the man covering him.

The play worked to perfection. Montana drew back, threw, and connected with wideout John Taylor in the end zone's center. The extra point was good, and the 49ers had a solid four-point lead. Only a Bengal touchdown would take the victory from San Francisco now — and with only 30 seconds left in the game, that seemed impossible.

It was. Fans everywhere who had prayed for a close game had certainly gotten more than they had bargained for. To this day, the last-minute San Francisco victory still rates as one of the most heart-stopping games in the history of professional football.

And the 49ers weren't done impressing people yet. They ended the next season with a 14–2 record and cruised their way into their fourth Super Bowl in eight years. They were being described as a dynasty, with Joe Montana as their king and Steve Young as the heir apparent.

Super Bowl XXIV would also see the return of another championship game veteran. The Denver Broncos had made two trips in the past three years and both times had come up lacking. They hoped that this, their third journey, would turn things around for them. Many football followers believed that for that to happen, quarterback John Elway would have to bring something special to the game.

The 49ers got off to a quick start, chalking up seven points in the first five minutes with a 20-yard pass from Montana to Jerry Rice. Then Elway worked his team into field-goal range. One kick later the score was 7–3.

After that, however, Elway and the Broncos began to falter. The quarterback's passes were coming up short time and again. Then they fumbled near the midfield line, and San Francisco recovered.

The 49ers were in firing range, and Montana didn't hesitate to pull the trigger. They scored another touchdown to put them ahead by ten after the extra-point kick missed.

Elway, meanwhile, was struggling. Out of ten pass attempts since the beginning of the game, he'd completed only two. Now his team was forced to punt because he failed to get a first down.

In comparison, when Montana took control again, he mounted an awesome attack that gave the 49ers 69 yards on 14 plays — and another 7 points. Then, with a mere 34 seconds left before the end of the half, he launched a 38-yard pass into the waiting hands of Jerry Rice, giving the 49ers 27 points to the Broncos 3.

Denver never recovered. While they managed to put another 7 points on the board, San Francisco ended the game with 55 points, the most any team had ever scored in a Super Bowl. The 45-point margin was also a new Super Bowl record — as were Joe Montana's stats. He had thrown for 297 yards, passed for 1,142, and led his team to 5 touchdowns. He had been sacked only once and, for the fourth time in his Super Bowl career, had not thrown a single interception. Not surprisingly, he was awarded his third MVP trophy.

On the flip side, the Broncos were staring at a record of their own: 4 trips to the Super Bowl, 4 Super Bowl losses.

"I'm just trying to figure out how we can win one of these one of these days," a frustrated Elway said after the game.

Many other teams had felt that same frustration in the past. But no one could have predicted that it would happen to the same team in the next four Super Bowls.

⋆ CHAPTER TEN ⋆

1991–1996

Repeat Defeats and the Rise of a New Dynasty

The Buffalo Bills had been a "close but no cigar" team for many years. In 1990, they finally trumped their competition to reach their first Super Bowl.

Their opponents were the New York Giants. The Giants had pulled off an enormous feat that year by besting the 49ers in the NFC championship. It remained to be seen if they could do the same to the Bills.

The game was played on January 27, 1991 — a mere twelve days after the United States had entered the Persian Gulf War in an attempt to stop Iraq's invasion of the small but oil-rich country of Kuwait. Citizens in the States were understandably on edge, worried that the war would unleash terrorist activity in their homeland.

In response, the NFL stepped up its usual security. It also chose to downplay the usual pregame and game-day shenanigans in favor of focusing on the game itself. They hoped the Super Bowl would provide a welcome relief from the tension the war was creating. For those fans who appreciated a close contest, the teams more than delivered.

The game promised to be a power struggle between defensive might and offensive power. In the past year, the Bills had scored more points per game than any other team in the league. The Giants, on the other hand, had allowed fewer points than any other team. So the question for many people was, would the Bills' offense be able to outmaneuver the Giants' defense?

At first, it seemed the answer was no. The Giants crushed the Bills' first touchdown attempt and then got on the board with a field goal. But the Bills came back quickly with three of their own to knot the score.

In the second quarter, the Bills drove their way into the end zone on twelve plays to go up by seven. Then they found two more points when the Bills pounced on the Giants' quarterback behind New York's goal line.

Not to be outdone, the Giants pounded the Bills with an 87-yard jaunt for their first touchdown. Going into the half, the score was 12–10.

It stayed that way for the first nine minutes of the third quarter. The Giants had possession of the ball that entire time — a Super Bowl record — and with 9:29 that had elapsed, finally managed to bull into the end zone. Now New York led, 17–12.

Throughout that nine-and-a-half-minute drive, the Bills' offense had been cooling their heels on the sidelines. When they finally came back on the field, they were ready for action. They pushed the Giants' defense hard and fast and gained another touchdown to take the lead, 19–17.

That lead melted away soon afterward, however. The Bills' defense had taken a pounding during the Giants' seemingly endless nine-minute drive; now they were expected to stop them again. But they couldn't. New York worked its way into field-goal range and, one kick later, the Giants had stolen the lead by one point.

There was still plenty of time left on the clock. If the Bills could score just one more time, they would win.

Slowly, they moved downfield until, with 48 seconds remaining, they were on New York's 46. Three plays later, they were on the 29.

With eight seconds showing on the clock, kicker Scott Norwood jogged onto the field. After the snap, Norwood drew back and connected. The ball soared end over end — and veered off to the right, missing the uprights by less than a foot!

The Giants leaped in triumph while the Bills slumped in defeat. Norwood took full blame for the loss. "I let a lot of people down tonight," he acknowledged.

Unfortunately for Bills' fans, it wouldn't be the last time they were let down by their team.

In late 1991, Buffalo reached their second consecutive Super Bowl. They wanted nothing more than to erase the previous year's defeat with a victory. Instead, they joined the ranks of two-time losers when they dropped Super Bowl XXVI to the Washington Redskins, 37 to 24.

Some believed the loss was caused by the season-long infighting that had plagued the Bills. Others said the team had been so confident in its abilities that it hadn't tried hard enough. And then there were those who realized that the Bills had simply been outsmarted. Whatever the reason, Buffalo left the game licking its wounds.

After two defeats in as many years, it was understandable that Bills fans expected more from their team when it reached the Super Bowl for the third year in a row. But once again, they were bitterly disappointed. In fact, Super Bowl XXVII was the Bills' worst defeat yet. Buffalo turned over the ball nine times in the 52–17 pasting by the newly resurrected Dallas Cowboys and their superstar quarterback, Troy Aikman.

The next season Dallas galloped ahead of the pack to reach the Super Bowl again. So too did the Buffalo Bills, to the surprise of many. Super Bowl XXVIII was a grudge match that pitted the three-time winners against the three-time losers. Troy Aikman, Emmitt Smith, and the rest of the Cowboys were eager to slip another Super Bowl ring onto their fingers. The Buffalo Bills, meanwhile, were still trying to cleanse the bitter taste of defeat from their mouths. This year, they hoped to sample the sweetness of victory instead.

The Cowboys won the toss and elected to receive. They returned the opening kickoff for 50 yards! The Bills held them to a three-point field goal, however, and soon tied it up with a field goal of their own — only to see the knot come unraveled when Dallas kicked a second field goal before the end of the first quarter.

Then, slowly, the game turned in favor of the Bills. Quarterback Jim Kelly got hot and, with a combination of handoffs and sharp passes, moved the ball to within 4 yards of Dallas's goal line. One play later, it was Buffalo 10, Dallas 6!

Buoyed by the turnaround, the Bills' defense caught fire. On the next series of plays, they intercepted an Aikman pass. Kelly took over and threaded together a run that put the Bills in field-goal range. With one solid kick, the Bills' lead jumped by three more points.

The score going into the locker room was 13–6 — much to the Cowboys' amazement. They had battered and bruised Buffalo the previous year and had expected to do nothing less this year.

The mood in Buffalo's locker room was much different. Was it possible that the thrice-denied Bills might actually win their first Super Bowl?

It was not. By the end of the third quarter, Dallas had regained the lead, 20–13. And by the end of the fourth, the Bills were once again left staring at the turf while the Cowboys celebrated their second consecutive and fourth overall Super Bowl victory, making them the third team in NFL history to achieve that milestone.

Buffalo had reached a milestone, too — the first team ever to lose four consecutive Super Bowls. Bills' players and fans agreed that that was an honor they would have preferred not to have. Quarterback Jim Kelly summed it up by simply stating, "It's frustrating, it really is."

★ CHAPTER ELEVEN ★

1995–1999

Battles for Dynastic Supremacy

By the mid-1990s, three NFL teams were acknowledged to be dynasties: the San Francisco 49ers, the Pittsburgh Steelers, and the Dallas Cowboys. They had all won four championships. Now the race was on to see which team would be the first to win five Super Bowl titles. Pittsburgh wore the crown, having won four Super Bowls, the other two teams were close behind with three apiece. Both Dallas and San Francisco were eager to tie Pittsburgh's record — and surpass it, if possible.

Since their last Super Bowl victory in 1990, the 49ers had experienced growing pains. In 1992, backup quarterback Steve Young took over for Joe Montana, only to have the job taken away from him again in 1993. Finally, in 1994, he regained his place after Montana moved to the Kansas City Chiefs. That year, Young took his team all the way.

The 49ers' opponents in Super Bowl XXIX were the surprising San Diego Chargers. A scrappy team, the Chargers had battled long and hard for the chance to compete in their first Super Bowl. Yet for all their pluck and determination, the Chargers were the underdogs — a fact the 49ers let them know a scant 90 seconds into the game.

San Francisco had received the kickoff and within two plays had brought the ball to San Diego's 44. On the next play, Young hit Jerry Rice with a pass. Rice charged past the Chargers into the end zone, earning the team six points and a place in the record books for the quickest TD ever made in a Super Bowl.

Three minutes later, the 49ers had made it 14–0. The Chargers answered with a touchdown of their own, but before the half, Young had found receivers in the end zone two more times to put the score at 28–7. A field goal finally put San Diego into double digits, but with an 18-point deficit, victory over the 49ers looked impossible.

Still, the Chargers had made a habit of coming

from behind that season, and there was still a whole half yet to be played.

Unfortunately for San Diego fans, San Francisco got to play in that half, too. They started it with a march down the field that ended in a touchdown. They scored again midway through the third quarter to put the game at 42 to 10.

The Chargers were sputtering, but they weren't out yet. They returned the kickoff an amazing 98 yards to post 6 more for their side, then added 2 more with a 2-point conversion. They added eight more again before the game's end, but it wasn't enough. The 49ers had boosted over the line one more time themselves to bring their final point total to 49.

With the win, San Francisco grabbed the top spot in Super Bowl history, with five victories. But when the next Super Bowl rolled around, they realized they were soon going to share that spot with another team. The only question was, which team would join them, the Dallas Cowboys or the Pittsburgh Steelers?

Pittsburgh and Dallas had met twice before, at Super Bowls X and XIII. Both times Pittsburgh had come away with the win. Dallas badly wanted to beat their nemesis — but Pittsburgh wanted the victory just as much. And of course both teams wanted to come away with their fifth Super Bowl win.

The Dallas Cowboys had won their third and fourth Super Bowls in 1993 and 1994. While they didn't make it to the big game the next year, in 1995 they had a phenomenal roster that included Troy Aikman, Emmitt Smith, and the newly acquired cornerback/receiver Deion "Prime Time" Sanders, formerly of the 49ers. Under their new coach, Barry Switzer, the Cowboys had built a record of 12–4 plus two post-season victories.

The Pittsburgh Steelers had been away from the Super Bowl since 1980. In the 15 years that had followed that victory, the team had seesawed between strong seasons and weak seasons. In 1995, however, they barreled back to the top of the AFC under the quarterbacking of Neil O'Donnell and receiving talents of Yancey Thigpen, Andre Hastings, and Ernie Mills. With rookie Kordell Stewart filling in as needed at quarterback, receiver, and running back, the Steelers looked better than they had in years.

Football followers predicted that this game would be won on the ground rather than in the air, as the passing games of both teams were secondary to their running and defensive games. Sure enough, the first points came from short passes and fierce runs. Sadly for Pittsburgh fans, all 13 of those points—two field goals and a touchdown—were made by the Cowboys.

But there was plenty of time left in the half, and the Steelers made good use of it. O'Donnell bulled his team down the field in the second quarter, reaching the Dallas 6. On the next play, he blasted a bullet pass to Thigpen to bring Pittsburgh within six of Dallas at the half.

The first half had been relatively mistake-free for both teams. The same was not true of the second half. Early in the third quarter, O'Donnell tried a soft pass close to the Dallas goal line. It was picked off and returned for 44 yards. The Cowboys scored two plays later, putting Dallas ahead 20 to 7.

The Steelers buckled down after that and held the Cowboys scoreless going into the fourth quarter. Dallas, on the other hand, allowed Pittsburgh to get within field-goal range. When the kick was good, the Steelers were only 10 points behind. O'Donnell moved forward again in a drive that ended with a

1-yard touchdown plunge to put the Steelers within easy reach of the lead.

Then disaster struck. O'Donnell threw another interception. The Cowboys returned it to the Pittsburgh 6-yard line. The Steelers tried to hold them there, but failed to stop Emmitt Smith. The Cowboys went ahead by ten points, a lead that proved insurmountable for the Steelers. The final score of Super Bowl XXX was 27–17.

The Cowboys were overjoyed at having finally bested the Steelers and at having tied the 49ers at five Super Bowl wins. Even those who had hoped for a Pittsburgh victory had to admit that Dallas had put together an impressive season. "They are a great, great team," said Chuck Noll, the man who had coached the Steelers to their four Super Bowl victories. "People think it is easy to do what they have done. But it isn't. Or more would have done it."

Long ago in football history, there had been another team many fans had thought of as a "great, great team" — the Green Bay Packers, winner of the first two Super Bowls. But nearly three decades had elapsed since those victories without the Packers coming out on top.

Then came the 1996 season. That year, the Packers vaulted ahead of the competition with a record of 13–3, thanks in large part to their hard-working quarterback Brett Favre. Now, 29 years after their last win, Green Bay was going to the Super Bowl.

Their opponents, the New England Patriots, were making their second appearance at the big game. They had lost out to the Chicago Bears in 1986 but now, with their talented young quarterback, Drew Bledsoe, and their powerhouse defense, they felt ready to take on the Packers.

But feeling ready and being ready are two different things; and on the Packers' second play of the game, the Patriots were caught napping. Favre read the signs of an oncoming blitz and quickly switched the play he had planned to call. With that audible, he turned a potential sack into a 54-yard touchdown.

Moments later, Bledsoe threw an interception. The Packers regained possession at the Patriots' 28-yard line and scored a field goal to make the score 10–0.

But New England answered with a touchdown of their own after a hard-hitting 79-yard drive. They added another seven before the end of the quarter to make it 14–10.

Favre punched back almost immediately with the longest-scoring play in Super Bowl history, an 81-yard pass reception to Antonio Freeman. The score was now 17–14, but it didn't stay that way for long. The Packers racked up 3 more on their side with another field goal and then broke away from the Pats even further by turning another Bledsoe interception into a touchdown. Going into the half, it was Green Bay 27, New England 14.

Bledsoe tightened up his passes in the second half and, with a combination of short shots and handoffs, managed to get his team within scoring distance. One 18-yard rush later, the Pats had drawn to within six. The touchdown had them completely stoked — until the next play, that is.

Packer Desmond Howard fielded New England's kickoff at the 1-yard line. Then he started to run. Down the field he went, dodging tackles and bouncing off defenders, until he had covered the entire length for a 99-yard touchdown! Insult was added to the Patriots' injury with a 2-point conversion, thus adding 9 points to the Packers' score in just one minute!

New England couldn't recover. By the game's end, Bledsoe had thrown 4 interceptions. In the second half alone he had been sacked 3 times. The day belonged to the Packers who, after three long decades, were once again the Super Bowl champs.

The next year saw Favre and the Packers reaching the Super Bowl once again. Many believed they would emerge victorious, if only because their opponents were the Denver Broncos.

Denver had knocked on the championship door four times before but each time had been turned away without a ring. John Elway, the Broncos' longtime quarterback, was considering retiring at the end of the 1997 season. A Super Bowl win would be the perfect sendoff. But to get the prize, he needed help.

Terrell "T.D." Davis had been with the Broncos since his rookie season in 1995, and in him, Elway had gotten just the help he needed. "Terrell has taken the pressure off me to throw on every down," Elway reported. "People have had to worry about not only our passing game but also our running game."

Davis proved just how dangerous he could be early on. Green Bay got on the board first with a 76-yard push that ended with a 22-yard, Favre-to-Freeman pass, but Denver answered with a long drive of its own that saw T.D. plunging from the 1-yard line to tie things up.

In the next quarter, Elway showed he still had plenty of razzle-dazzle left in him. The Broncos intercepted a Favre pass and drove all the way to the Packers' 1. On the next play, Elway faked a pass to Davis and then rolled into the end zone himself. Now the Broncos had the upper hand with a 14 to 7 lead. And when the Packers fumbled soon after, they took advantage and added three more with a field goal.

Then the Broncos took a blow to their offense. Davis, who had suffered from migraines for years, went to the locker room with a blinding headache. While he was out, Green Bay added a touchdown to come within three.

Luckily for Denver, Davis returned to the lineup for the second half. Even though he was not fully recovered — a dropped pitchout on the first play showed that — he slowly regained his strength, and soon he was ramming his way through Green Bay's defense again. A 21-yard gain was followed by another 1-yard plunge for his second touchdown of the game. And in the fourth quarter he did it again, giving the Broncos a 31–24 lead over the Packers — and their very first Super Bowl victory.

Elway was beside himself with happiness. "It feels two times better than I could have imagined," he said. "I have wiped the slate clean." With the win, the Broncos had not only ended their four-time losing streak, they had given the AFC its first victory over the NFC in 13 years. "To finally come out and show the NFC and everyone, it's unbelievable," Elway said.

The quarterback put his decision to retire to bed, choosing instead to play on for one more year. And for that, the Broncos would be forever grateful, because in January 1998 they celebrated another winning season and their second consecutive trip to the Super Bowl to play the Atlanta Falcons.

Elway would have reason to celebrate after Super Bowl XXXIII. That game, he threw 29 passes. Eighteen of those were complete, and one went 80 yards for a touchdown. He made a touchdown, too, hurtling himself across the goal line from 3 yards out.

Those 2 TDs, plus 2 more and 2 field goals, gave the Broncos 34 points. The Falcons, on the other hand, put up only 19. After losing four Super Bowls, Denver and Elway had now won two in a row. For his efforts, Elway was named MVP.

"I never thought it could get any better than last year," he enthused after the game.

⋆ CHAPTER TWELVE ⋆

2000–2006

Into the New Millennium

The Super Bowl turned thirty-four years old at the turn of the century. In its lifetime it had seen the rise of superstar athletes and team dynasties. It had witnessed controversial calls and career-ending injuries. It had produced heart-wrenching defeats and heart-stopping victories. But for the first time, in the year 2000, it would see two relatively unknown teams vying for a place among the winners.

The Tennessee Titans and the St. Louis Rams had been in the NFL for generations, but both had shifted hometowns and changed names more than once, leaving would-be fans behind. Now each hoped to make a permanent mark by winning the first Super Bowl of the new millennium.

The game combined all the best the Super Bowl

had to offer. There was fantastic quarterbacking by two new faces, the Rams' Kurt Warner and the Titans' Steve McNair. The offenses put together several astonishing catches and runs while the defenses punished those in their path time and again. The score seesawed back and forth until, with just two minutes left to go, it was tied at 16 apiece. An overtime decision seemed inevitable.

Instead, viewers were treated to one of the most exciting football endings in Super Bowl history. The Rams had the ball on their own 27-yard line. With the clock ticking down, Warner took the snap and faded back. At the same time, Titan Jevon Kearse plowed his way through, making a beeline for the quarterback. Whatever play Warner had hoped to make was about to end in either a sack or a blocked pass.

Or was it? Moments before Kearse hit him, Warner hurled the ball downfield. Rams receiver Isaac Bruce saw the ball spiral in the air. He did what any good player would do — he ran to get under it. Then he did what few players with the ball can do — he freed himself from three defenders and ran the length of the field for a touchdown. The whole play had taken only seconds, but now the Rams were up by seven.

There was still time on the clock, however, and the Titans used it to drive their way deep into the Rams' territory. At the 10-yard line, there was time enough for one last "miracle" play.

But the miracle never came. While McNair connected with his intended receiver, Kevin Dyson, Ram linebacker Mike Jones wrapped his arms around Dyson's legs. As Dyson fell, he stretched out his arm, hoping the ball in his hand would pass the goal line. It didn't. The game ended with the Rams winning 23 to 16.

On the heels of such a thrilling finale, Super Bowl XXXV between the New York Giants and the Baltimore Ravens came across as a bit dull. The Ravens had a defense so strong that they kept the Giants mired in their own territory throughout the second half. Meanwhile, their offense ran circles around the Giants defense. The game ended with Baltimore crushing New York, 34 to 7.

The following year saw the return of the St. Louis Rams and quarterback Kurt Warner. The last time the Rams had played in the Super Bowl they had faced a team of equal strength and won in the final minutes. This time, they would meet the New England Patriots, a team that most considered far inferior to the Rams.

The Pats had had a troubling beginning to their season, dropping their first two games and then losing their star quarterback, Drew Bledsoe, to injury. But the second-string QB, Tom Brady, more than filled Bledsoe's shoes. The team also saw the rise of new and former players, including receiver Troy Brown and rusher Antowain Smith. Coach Bill Belichick put together a complicated defense system; once the Pats had mastered it, they used it to great advantage.

That defense hit the Rams hard early in Super Bowl XXXVI and managed to limit the best offense in the league to a single field goal. Warner took a hard hit at one point and injured the thumb on his throwing hand. He stayed in the game despite the pain and in the second quarter threw an interception that was returned 47 yards for a New England touchdown.

The Pats sweetened their 7–3 lead with 7 more

just before halftime, and by the end of the third quarter had added 3 more to make it 17–3. But the Rams came pounding back. First Warner pushed his team to the 2-yard line and racked up seven points by crossing into the end zone himself. Then he threw a 26-yard touchdown pass to tie the game at 17 apiece — with 90 seconds left on the clock!

No Super Bowl had ever gone into overtime before, but everyone watching believed this one would. Not everyone in the game thought so, though. Despite the fact that the kickoff found the Pats on their own 17-yard line, Coach Belichick told Brady to go for the win.

Brady did. Short pass after short pass, he worked the New England offense down the field, from their 17 to the Rams' 31. The clock, meanwhile, ticked down from ninety seconds to seven.

That's where it stayed while Patriots kicker Adam Vinatieri ran on for a field goal attempt. It was the most important kick of his life, but Vinatieri was used to pressure. When the ball was placed, he calmly kicked it through the uprights to give the Patriots their first Super Bowl win. Tom Brady, who had thrown only three passes the previous season, was awarded MVP honors for his outstanding game. When asked to comment on his role in the victory, he refused to take credit. "My team is why I'm here. My team is why we won the Super Bowl ring."

The ring would go to a different team the following year. Like the Patriots, the Tampa Bay Buccaneers had an outstanding defense. In Super Bowl XXXVII, they completely mowed down the Oakland Raiders' offense, holding them to just 3 points in the first half while their own offense racked up 20. Along the way to their 48–21 victory, the Bucs sacked quarterback Rich Gannon five times, intercepted five of his passes — three of which were returned for touchdowns — and ran up 34 unanswered points.

The next year saw the return of the New England Patriots, this time facing off against the Carolina Panthers. The Pats were coming off an amazing 14–2 regular season, but the Panthers had had a strong year as well, finishing 11–5.

The first quarter went scoreless as the two teams battled it out defensively. Then, at nearly twelve minutes into the second quarter, the Patriots got on the board with a 5-yard pass from Brady to Deion

Branch. The kick was good, and the Pats were up by seven.

Carolina answered less than two minutes later with their own TD and extra-point conversion, only to see the tie vanish 49 seconds after that when Brady again found a receiver in the end zone. The Panthers then managed to draw within four before the half on a field goal.

The third period went scoreless. But 11 seconds into the fourth, the Patriots added 7 to their side with a 71-yard drive.

The Panthers clawed their way to another touchdown midway through the fourth quarter, too. Then, with New England in prime scoring position, the Panthers intercepted Brady's third-and-goal pass. On their next possession, quarterback Jake Delhomme lofted a Super Bowl record 85-yard touchdown pass to give the Panthers a one-point lead. With the score at 22–21, there was less than seven minutes left on the clock.

Undaunted, the Patriots drove deep into Carolina territory, moving the ball 68 yards in one possession and then bulling into the end zone from the 1-yard line to make it 27 to 22. They went for the two-point conversion on the next play — and got it to make the score 29 to 22 with less than three minutes to go.

Unbelievably, Carolina scored again two minutes later. Now the clock showed 1:08, the scoreboard 29–29. An overtime decision seemed inevitable, but then New England got a break. The kickoff went out of bounds, automatically bringing the ball to the Patriots' 40. From there, Brady marched his team to the opposite 40. At third down and three to go, there were 14 seconds left on the clock. To avoid overtime, Brady had to get the ball into scoring range. He did just that, rifling a 17-yard pass to Branch.

Adam Vinatieri hurried onto the field. It was an eerily familiar situation: two years ago he had made the game-winning field goal. This Super Bowl, however, he had missed one, had one blocked, and made one. What would happen when his foot connected this time?

What happened was the stuff that puts the "super" into Super Bowl. Vinatieri lofted for a 41-yard field goal. The Patriots were once again Super Bowl champs!

"There is no better feeling in the world," wide

receiver Troy Brown enthused after the game. "This one is even better than the first. Ten times better than the first."

But as good as that second one felt, the third one felt even better. February 6, 2005, found the New England Patriots winning Super Bowl XXXIX. In four years, they had won the big game three times; only the Dallas Cowboys had accomplished as much at the height of their NFL domination. Tom Brady joined the ranks of Terry Bradshaw, Troy Aikman, and Joe Montana as a three-time Super Bowl–winning quarterback — and at 27, he was the youngest to reach that milestone.

Like their previous two Super Bowl wins, the victory over the Philadelphia Eagles came down to the wire. The first quarter was scoreless. The second saw the Eagles getting on first with 7 but the Patriots tying it up before the half. Four minutes into the third period New England added 7 more. Philadelphia responded by posting 7 of their own. Nine plays into the last quarter the Pats jumped ahead again on another touchdown. A Vinatieri field goal followed that TD to give the Patriots a 24-to-14 lead.

The Eagles pushed as hard as they could and drew within three points with less than 2 minutes left on the clock. To win the game, however, they had to stop New England's drive and regain possession. They did just that, but there was only 49 seconds to go. Try as they might, they just couldn't move the ball quickly enough. The Patriots won 24–21.

Tom Brady's numbers were outstanding once again, with 23 pass completions, 2 touchdown passes, and a total of 236 yards. But it was Deion Branch who came away with the MVP trophy, thanks to his Super Bowl record–tying 11 catches for 133 yards.

When asked how he felt about the award, Branch replied, "I'm just so thankful to be a part of this team. . . . It didn't make any difference who won the MVP. I just think we all wanted to win this game. . . . We just wanted to come out and prove that we can win another Super Bowl."

The Patriots and New England fans had high hopes that they would walk home with another Vince Lombardi trophy the following year. Instead, the Pittsburgh Steelers bulled their way to Super Bowl XL with victories in three tough away games in the post-season. The Seattle Seahawks also sprinted past their opponents to earn their first appearance in the big game.

Super Bowl XL took place on February 5, 2006, in Detroit. The game was scoreless until Seattle's quarterback, Matt Hasselbeck, threw a sixteen yard touchdown pass to Darrell Jackson. Unfortunately, the touchdown was nullified a moment later with a call of pass interference against the offense. Instead of seven points, the Seahawks had to settle for a three-point field goal.

Pittsburgh, meanwhile, was struggling to make a first down. They finally got it nineteen minutes into the game only to give the ball away on a pass interception. Luckily for the Steelers, the Seahawks failed to move the ball the required ten yards and they regained possession.

On the next series, quarterback Ben Roethlisberger battled back from penalty and a sack to drive his team to the Seattle 1-yard line. Two plays later, he punched his way into the end zone.

Or did he? Mike Holmgren, the Seahawks head coach, challenged the touchdown, saying that Roethlisberger hadn't carried the ball across. After reviewing the play, however, the umpires ruled the touchdown good — and the Steelers were up by four.

The score stayed at 7–3 going into the second half. So far, neither team had done much to excite the fans. That changed six seconds into the third quarter. Roethlisberger passed off to running back Willie Parker. Parker broke loose and ran 75 yards for a touchdown, breaking a record set by Marcus Allen in Super Bowl XVIII. The Steelers were up 14–3.

The Seahawks came close to narrowing that margin on their next possession. Then the touchdown drive faltered and the field goal attempt was no good. Seattle fans were beginning to despair.

But their despair turned to hope again when, on the Steelers' next drive, Roethlisberger threw an interception into the arms of Kelly Herndon. Herndon sprinted 76 yards downfield, breaking another Super Bowl record for the longest interception return. One minute later, Hasselbeck threw a 16-yard touchdown pass and suddenly, the Seahawks were only behind by four.

Seattle rode the momentum of that touchdown into the fourth quarter. Hasselbeck pushed his team deep into Pittsburgh territory. Five minutes into the quarter, another TD was within their reach.

But the chance slipped through their fingers when a pass intended for Darrell Jackson was intercepted by Ike Taylor. Adding insult to injury, Hasselbeck was penalized fifteen yards for throwing an illegal low block.

Pittsburgh took control at their 44-yard line. A minute later they were at the Seattle 43. Then came the play that sealed the Steelers' victory while simultaneously delighting fans.

Roethlisberger took the snap and quickly pitched the ball to Parker on his left. Parker ran toward right field and passed off to Antwaan Randle El. Randle El then fired off a pass to Hines Ward. A few steps later and Ward danced into the end zone!

The Seahawks worked hard to make up the eleven-point differential, but it was no use. The final score of Super Bowl XL was Pittsburgh 21, Seattle 10.

The Steelers and their fans went wild. The victory

gave the players "one for the thumb" — a slogan referring to the digit their fifth Super Bowl ring would adorn. Roethlisberger became the youngest quarterback ever to win the Super Bowl and Ward was awarded MVP.

The win was especially sweet for coach Bill Cowher as it silenced critics who claimed he didn't have what it took to guide a team to Super Bowl victory. A grinning Cowher handed owner Dan Rooney the Lombardi trophy, saying, "I've been waiting a long time to do this." But for many, it was Jerome Bettis ("The Bus") who stole the show when he announced his retirement after the game.

"It's been an incredible ride," he said, flashing a smile well-known to his fans.

"An incredible ride" sums up the past forty years of Super Bowl history as well. How else to describe the meteoric rise of this game, from its infancy as a contest between warring leagues, to its place as one of the most anticipated sporting events in the world? These decades have given us classic moments to remember and revisit; talented, driven players to hang our hopes on; and teams that excite our loyalty even when they suffer defeat. For many, this Sunday championship has become an American tradition, an annual celebration of a hard-hitting, fast-action sport born and raised in this country.

Incredible, indeed.

Super Bowl Results

Game	Date	Result
I	January 15, 1967	Green Bay 35, Kansas City 10
II	January 14, 1968	Green Bay 33, Oakland 14
III	January 12, 1969	N.Y. Jets 16, Baltimore 7
IV	January 11, 1970	Kansas City 23, Minnesota 7
V	January 17, 1971	Baltimore 16, Dallas 13
VI	January 16, 1972	Dallas 24, Miami 3
VII	January 14, 1973	Miami 14, Washington 7
VIII	January 13, 1974	Miami 24, Minnesota 7
IX	January 12, 1975	Pittsburgh 16, Minnesota 6
X	January 18, 1976	Pittsburgh 21, Dallas 17
XI	January 9, 1977	Oakland 32, Minnesota 14
XII	January 15, 1978	Dallas 27, Denver 10
XIII	January 21, 1979	Pittsburgh 35, Dallas 31
XIV	January 20, 1980	Pittsburgh 31, L.A. Rams 19
XV	January 25, 1981	Oakland 27, Philadelphia 10
XVI	January 24, 1982	San Francisco 26, Cincinnati 21
XVII	January 30, 1983	Washington 27, Miami 17
XVIII	January 22, 1984	L.A. Raiders 38, Washington 9
XIX	January 20, 1985	San Francisco 38, Miami 16
XX	January 26, 1986	Chicago 46, New England 10
XXI	January 25, 1987	N.Y. Giants 39, Denver 20

XXII	January 31, 1988	Washington 42, Denver 10
XXIII	January 22, 1989	San Francisco 20, Cincinnati 16
XXIV	January 28, 1990	San Francisco 55, Denver 10
XXV	January 27, 1991	N.Y. Giants 20, Buffalo 19
XXVI	January 26, 1992	Washington 37, Buffalo 24
XXVII	January 31, 1993	Dallas 52, Buffalo 17
XXVIII	January 30, 1994	Dallas 30, Buffalo 13
XXIX	January 29, 1995	San Francisco 49, San Diego 26
XXX	January 28, 1996	Dallas 27, Pittsburgh 17
XXXI	January 26, 1997	Green Bay 35, New England 21
XXXII	January 25, 1998	Denver 31, Green Bay 24
XXXIII	January 31, 1999	Denver 34, Atlanta 19
XXXIV	January 30, 2000	St. Louis 23, Tennessee 16
XXXV	January 28, 2001	Baltimore 34, N.Y. Giants 7
XXXVI	February 3, 2002	New England 20, St. Louis 17
XXXVII	January 26, 2003	Tampa Bay 48, Oakland 21
XXXVIII	February 1, 2004	New England 32, Carolina 29
XXXIX	February 6, 2005	New England 24, Philadelphia 21
XL	February 5, 2006	Pittsburgh 21, Seattle 10

Teams That Have Won Three or More Super Bowls

Dallas Cowboys (1972, 1978, 1993, 1994, 1996)
San Francisco 49ers (1982, 1985, 1989, 1990, 1995)
Pittsburgh Steelers (1975, 1976, 1979, 1980)
New England Patriots (2002, 2004, 2005)
Washington Redskins (1983, 1988, 1992)
Green Bay Packers (1967, 1968, 1997)

Matt Christopher®

Muhammad Ali

Lance Armstrong

Kobe Bryant

Jennifer Capriati

Jeff Gordon

Ken Griffey Jr.

Mia Hamm

Tony Hawk

Ichiro

Derek Jeter

Randy Johnson

Michael Jordan

Mario Lemieux

Tara Lipinski

Mark McGwire

Yao Ming

Shaquille O'Neal

Jackie Robinson

Alex Rodriguez

Babe Ruth

Curt Schilling

Sammy Sosa

Venus and Serena Williams

Tiger Woods

The #1 Sports Series for Kids

Read them all!

Baseball Pals

Baseball Turnaround

The Basket Counts

Body Check

Catch That Pass!

Catcher with a Glass Arm

Catching Waves

Center Court Sting

Centerfield Ballhawk

Challenge at Second Base

The Comeback Challenge

Comeback of the Home Run Kid

Cool as Ice

The Diamond Champs

Dirt Bike Racer

Dirt Bike Runaway

Dive Right In

Double Play at Short

Face-Off

Fairway Phenom

Football Fugitive

Football Nightmare

The Fox Steals Home

Goalkeeper in Charge

The Great Quarterback Switch

Halfback Attack*

The Hockey Machine

Ice Magic

Inline Skater

Johnny Long Legs

The Kid Who Only Hit Homers

Lacrosse Face-Off

*Previously published as Crackerjack Halfback

Line Drive to Short**

Long-Arm Quarterback

Long Shot for Paul

Look Who's Playing First Base

Miracle at the Plate

Mountain Bike Mania

No Arm in Left Field

Nothin' But Net

Penalty Shot

Prime-Time Pitcher

Red-Hot Hightops

The Reluctant Pitcher

Return of the Home Run Kid

Roller Hockey Radicals

Run For It

Shoot for the Hoop

Shortstop from Tokyo

Skateboard Renegade

Skateboard Tough

Slam Dunk

Snowboard Champ

Snowboard Maverick

Snowboard Showdown

Soccer Duel

Soccer Halfback

Soccer Scoop

Stealing Home

The Submarine Pitch

The Team That Couldn't Lose

Tennis Ace

Tight End

Top Wing

Touchdown for Tommy

Tough to Tackle

Wheel Wizards

Windmill Windup

Wingman on Ice

The Year Mom Won the Pennant

All available in paperback from Little, Brown and Company

**Previously published as Pressure Play